Time Tra

Frank Belknap Long

Alpha Editions

This edition published in 2023

ISBN : 9789357937535

Design and Setting By
Alpha Editions
www.alphaedis.com
Email - info@alphaedis.com

Contents

TIME TRAP

BY FRANK BELKNAP LONG

Somebody waited for old Charley Grimes,
plodding across that darkside Luna
crater—somebody who couldn't exist.

Charley Grimes was a big man who had been everywhere in
the Solar System and collected trophies which were as strange
and shining as the stories he liked to tell.

His face was as gaunt as the jungle mask and, when he lit a pipe
and smoked it, you watched to see where the smoke would
drift. It wasn't hard to picture it drifting over the mountains of
the moon or across the flat red plains of Mars.

We were sitting around a campfire in the Rockies just as our
ancestors must have sat five hundred years in the past. We
were swapping yarns to get Charley started, and watching the
sun sink to rest on clouds shaped like wild mustangs when the
talk drifted to the dark side of the moon.

You know what it's like on the dark side. The brittle stars shine
down and the great craters loom up, but when you're flying
low in a rocket ship about all you can see through the viewpane
is a circle of radiance spotlighting a desolation as bleak as the
Siberian Steppes.

You miss so many things you don't dare even think about the
earth. If you're an escapist you cover your bunk with pictures
of the lush Venusian jungles and pretend you're somewhere
else. But if you're a realist you go outside and come to grips
with the bleakness in one way or another.

Charley was a realist.

"So I went wandering off just to see what I could find!"
Charley said.

We watched him get up, throw another log on the fire and draw his Indian blanket around himself—so tightly he looked like a great swathed mummy swaying in the glare.

"Nothing tremendous ever happens when you go exploring with all the trimmings!" Charley went on. "You've got to be devil-may-care about it. So I just made sure my helmet was screwed on tight and went striding away from the ship like a clockwork orang-outang!

"If you've been on the dark side you know that there's a sensation of bitter cold at all times—even when you're bundled up and in motion. You keep looking back and wishing you hadn't—and before you can count the stars in a square foot of sky you're at the bottom of a valley with glacial sides and the desolation is so awful you want to sit down on the nearest rock and never get up!"

Charley sat down, crossed his long legs and took a deep, slow puff on his pipe.

"I shouted—just to hear the echoes come rolling back. You can talk to yourself that way and get comfort out of it, because what you'll hear will be the giant in yourself. The valley was so big a soaring eagle would have burst its lungs trying to fly out of it.

"But don't get the idea I climbed down over an icy slope on a rope. I simply sat down and let myself slide. Smooth? There wasn't a crevice or a projection until I reached the bottom and picked myself up."

Charley nodded. "I had to lift off my helmet for a minute, to shake off the ice. That's when I shouted and heard the echoes come rolling back.

"I'd clamped the helmet back on, and was adjusting my oxygen intake when I happened to glance down at my big, square feet."

Charley chuckled.

"I've got outsized feet even when I'm as bare as a baby. But I was wearing heavy moon-shoes, and the prints I'd left in the snow were eight inches across!

"There was a straight line of prints, as big and square as my own, leading out across the valley—prints I couldn't possibly have made. I'd stumbled around a bit, of course. But I hadn't budged two yards from the base of the slope.

"The oddest thing about that single trail of prints was the fact that it started right where I was standing!

"An icy wind seemed to blow through me. On the moon you don't slide down a steep slope and land right where someone else has been standing. Not if you're in your right mind, you don't. The moon isn't that thickly populated.

"I was badly shaken, I can tell you! But I didn't sit down and brood over it. When you go into a huddle with yourself on the moon you're apt to wind up looking like an ice-carved replica of Rodin's Thinker.

"I simply shaded my helmet with my palm, to cut down the starshine, and stared across the valley. The valley was about a mile wide, and as smooth as a skating rink over most of its surface. But about halfway across a big mound of blue-gray sandstone broke the monotony by looming up on the frozen plain like an African termite's nest.

"Maybe you've seen some pictures of those big nests in travel books. They were usually photographed with seven-foot natives standing beside 'em, to make you realize what insects could accomplish. Old travel books, of course, because Africa is just one big stone highway now.

"Those nests were huge, weren't they? If my memory doesn't betray me—some of those nests were twelve feet tall.

"Uh ... Uh. But this mound would have dwarfed twenty termite nests in a valley of giants—all tumbled together and piled up in a skyward direction.

"As near as I could make out the footprints ran right up to the base of the mound, and stopped there.

"Well ... you can be sure I didn't just stand in my own prints goggling up at the stars. I followed that impossible trail—straight out into the valley as fast as I could clump.

"It took me about ten minutes to reach the mound. Once or twice I stumbled and almost went sprawling. But whenever I felt the plain slipping out from under me I shot a quick glance at the mound and its sheer massiveness steadied me.

"Close up it had a corrugated, hoary look, as if it had bubbled up out of the ground when the moon had a molten crust and been fused into a mound by fire and earthquake.

"But when I halted directly in front of it I saw that it wasn't as solid as it looked. It was riddled with little dark holes, as though a woodpecker had spent at least a month making a wreck of it. And at its base there was a wide, dark, tunnel-like opening.

"Another man might have thought of a hundred excuses for not crawling through that tunnel on his hands and knees. But when my curiosity is aroused I'm a very special kind of idiot.

"The tunnel was about twenty feet in length. I crawled along through the darkness with my atomic blaster slapping against my hip, my heart hammering against my ribs.

"When the smothering feeling you get in tunnels began to wear thin I knew that it would be safe for me to stand up. You can feel a stone wall arching above you without touching it, and I knew suddenly that I was in the clear.

"When I got to my feet and stared about me I could see the dark end of the tunnel and what appeared to be stone walls hemming me in. The walls arched away into shadows, and were faintly luminous.

"I've spent as many hours underground as there are seeds in a watermelon—so I can take a cave interior in my stride. But the mound wasn't just hollow and cavelike and filled with wavering shadows. It was—occupied!

"He was sitting on a projecting ledge in deep shadows. But the wall behind him glowed, and I could see him clearly. He was wearing a space-suit exactly like my own, but it was all shriveled up over him.

"Take a little monkey—a lemur or a spectral tarsier will do—and put him inside a cumbersome space-suit, and let his bright eyes shine out through the viewpane. Do that—and you'll have as clear a picture of him as I could give you if I rambled on for ten minutes.

"I couldn't see the little fellow's face through the pane. It was all a shadowy blue. But I could see his bright eyes, and I could tell he was little by the way the suit overlapped, and bulged out in the wrong places.

"You know how a kid of eight or ten looks when he puts on a man's suit on Hallowe'en? But this wasn't Hallowe'en, and he wasn't trying to scare anyone!

"He was too scared himself. He was shaking all over and when he saw me his eyes got even brighter, and he started to get up. He was trembling so I had to help him to his feet.

"I steadied him with one arm and lifted off the helmet with my free hand. As you know, you can stay outside a suit on the moon without getting frost-bitten for about half a minute.

"When his face came into view and his eyes looked straight into mine I was so startled that fifteen seconds were lost right at the start—before a single word could be exchanged between us. But at least I had a chance to get a good look at him.

"If you saw yourself as a boy of ten, suddenly, without warning, would you recognize yourself? Maybe some men would. If you looked at yourself a lot in a mirror when you were growing up—or kept photographs of yourself, carefully preserved in an old album, you might not have any trouble. Right off you might hear yourself muttering, 'Why, that's *me*!'

"But I had trouble. The kid's face was just enough like my own to give me a start. But I couldn't really place it—couldn't remember where I had seen it before.

"Then the kid spoke. 'I—I thought you were Pops! But you're not! He's older! Where am I? How did I get here?'

"The voice did something to me. You get a chance to hear yourself talking a lot when you're knee-high to a grasshopper. And I had no kids of my own! But my own father had looked enough like me to be my twin brother, and if this kid thought I was his dad—

"It hit me between the eyes—and like a voice screaming at me through a blur of spinning suns!

"I was staring at myself as I had been long ago—and no tracks made by a dead man in a bog could have been more nerve-shattering.

"He wasn't even a poor little kid in a desperate plight, because you can't feel paternal about yourself! He was a tormented ghost out of the past, and for an instant I had an impulse to blame him and rail at him for returning to torture me.

"But I'm not a cruel man, deep down, and that crazy impulse passed quickly. He was a poor little lost cuss, even if he *was* myself, and all my sympathy went out to him.

"I even forgot for a moment how insane the whole thing was. He was gasping for breath, so I put the helmet back on, and gave the oxygen tube a double twist to straighten it out. But an instant before the helmet descended over his mouth he managed to stammer, 'I was up in the attic playing—'

"Playing 'Pirate's den!' I had spent the happiest years of my boyhood in the attic, pretending I was Captain Kidd, or climbing out on the tree that arched over our house when the December snows weighed it down, and making myself out to be in the crow's nest of an arctic windjammer!

"As I swayed there beside myself my mind followed crazy-paved paths in all directions. Great chunks of the past seemed to float before me—like icebergs nine-tenths submerged.

"But all the while the sanest part of my mind was seeking an explanation that would one-tenth explain it! I gripped my own boy-self by the shoulder to make sure he'd stay solid until the man he'd become could get a mental toe-hold on the problem.

"If you can persuade a man to mount a stepladder and plant himself firmly on the air you've taken your first brave step into the unknown. The poor devil may or may not fall. But at least you've made a start in the right direction.

"It isn't too hard to believe that certain things can happen to Time on the wrong side of yesterday—or tomorrow! Time—the physicists tell us—never stops flowing. It's like a melting candle or silk before it hardens on the loom—all crinkled up and sparkling like a dew-drenched spider web.

"If Time melts in a back-of-yesterday dimension what's to stop a man from dissolving with it, and running in a thin trickle back to his yesterdays? You were a boy once and you could be a boy again—without ceasing to be a man.

"Put it this way. On the dark side of the moon there was a valley of shadows. A big, blundering fool went stumbling into it, and landed in a heap. Before he could pick himself up a part of himself dissolved in some unimaginable backwash of time, and he became a boy again. His boy-self split off from him, and went stumbling off over the plain in a suit five sizes too large for him.

"It's not as impossible as it sounds. The boy you were still exists in Time, and he could emerge from the past to stand beside you in a vortex of dissolving Time. Was there something in the valley that could change the flow of time, reverse it, and twist it around like butter in a churn?

"The answer was right there in the cave with me. But I couldn't see it because *another* space-suited figure was making my brain whirl. He'd come clumping into the cave bent nearly double, and now he was shuffling toward me as though I'd committed some horrible crime I could never hope to atone for.

"Through the pane of his helmet his eyes burned accusingly into mine. But it wasn't until he halted directly in front of me and lifted the helmet from his head that I knew what my crime was and why he found it hard to forgive me.

"I had committed the crime of living beyond my alloted span! The man facing me was old ... old. His face was still my face, but if ever I had been young and handsome and a target for the wiles of a pretty woman I was so no longer!

"He seemed to realize that I could hardly bear to look upon myself as I would be, for he spoke sharply, quickly, without attempting to explain his presence, or even to prepare me for what he had to say by working up to it like a story-teller with a great load of unimaginable horror on his mind.

"'It's a monstrous beast of prey!' he croaked. 'It can dissolve Time and re-shape Time in a hundred horrible ways!'

"He quirked his head at me. 'You know more than that lad but I know more than you—for I have lived through this moment before! Once long ago I stood in this cave and warned you! You are at the crossroads of a branching future! If you take the right turn now you will live to become me. But, if you take the wrong turn—'

"He straightened, and pointed with his gloved forefinger into the shadows behind me. 'It is there—at your back! When you turn you will see the shining web which it uses to dissolve Time! All over this valley the creature has thrown a Time-dissolving web of force!'

"His voice rose warningly. 'It is as intelligent as we are, but it moves with glacial slowness. An inch in an hour—a foot in a day! When it dissolves Time it nourishes itself by drawing the energy-whirl into itself, and spinning it out again in another form, like an immense, living shuttlecock. A spider—'

"He looked at me with a haggard intensity of appeal. 'It will try to hold you with the web—to hold you in complete helplessness until you become a hundred lads and a hundred men. You'll be an infant, a boy of five, a lad of twenty, and a man older than myself. But every time you split up in the folds of the web you'll lose a part of your substance.

"'You'll cease to be a man with a past and a future. You'll become a mere hollow shell—no more substantial than I am, and I am little more than a wraith. You'll be drained, and you'll vanish like a puff of smoke. You'll be devoured and swallowed up!'

"He was struggling for breath and the veins on his forehead had begun to swell. 'You've got to blast it down before the web dazzles and confuses you! You'll have to face it to blast, but if you fight it with your mind—'

"Suddenly the helmet was back on his head and he was turning from me. He moved straight toward the lad and put a palsied hand on the shoulder of that younger me.

"Then, slowly, they both turned to face me, and I could see their eyes inside their helmets, trained upon me in desperate appeal. At least—there was appeal in the eyes of the old one. The lad may have been merely terrified, and confused.

"He couldn't have been more terrified than I was as the shadows lengthened about me, and a coldness crept into my bones.

"I knew I'd have to come to grips with the web. I knew, too, that if it was behind me I'd be safer facing it. When there's something unspeakable at your back, you can die so many deaths just waiting for it to make its presence known that all the courage and decision goes out of you.

"Panic smote me as I turned, hip and thigh like a flat sword. But all I could see for an instant was a faint, moving radiance blending with the shadows, a kind of nebulous flowing in the darkness on the far side of the cave.

"My hand must have closed on my blaster, for I could feel the bite of cold metal against my palm. But there was something about the light that my will could not withstand. My arms seemed to freeze as I stared at it, and terrifying thoughts rushed into my brain.

My arms seemed to freeze!

"At first I experienced only a feeling of almost unbearable oppression. Then something in the glow seemed to reach out toward me and there was no sound in the cave but the beating of my heart.

"A ghastly something seemed to be watching me with a kind of fiendish triumph, as though the soul of a devil lurked in the depth of the light which could send out vampire tendrils, filmed with writhing menace.

"I couldn't tear my eyes from the glow and the longer I stared the worse it got.

"The light seemed filled with an evil purpose. It writhed and changed shape as I stared at it, seeming to sweep out through the walls of the cave and back again with a pulsing greediness.

"Then, gradually, it ceased to blend with the shadows. It became stationary and transparent, hanging suspended in the murky air like a gigantic burning glass.

"As though in a dream-delirium I became slowly aware that a picture was forming within it. A valley swept into view, walled with high, saw-toothed mountain ranges.

"Deep in the weaving radiance I could see a tiny, plodding figure coming toward me across the valley.

"For an instant I thought I was looking at the far-off image of a human figure plodding over the plain. A figure clad in a heavy space-suit, moving awkwardly—as I had moved.

"Nearer it came and nearer, its reflection floating on ahead of it, bobbing about like a little ship.

"And then, suddenly, I saw that it was *skimming* the plain. It was balancing itself on flapping wings, sweeping across the plain without actually touching it, but so slowly that it appeared to be advancing with the plodding, awkward gait of a man.

"It swerved abruptly as I stared, made a full turn, and soared into the air. It flew straight toward me, its wings beating the air as though it were struggling against a furious uprush of wind.

"There was a sloping wall of light-dappled rock at the edge of the radiance, and for an instant the winged shape disappeared behind it. I didn't see it descend.

"I saw only a shadow forming behind the rock, and swirling out from it. It came into view again abruptly, dragging its wings behind it, hobbling toward me over the ice.

"My spine congealed. The thing that had crossed the valley was a monstrous bird of prey. It was wearing a space-suit, but no helmet, and I could see its vulture-like head bobbing about in the glow.

"It seemed to be in pain. It had halted at the edge of the glow, as if fearful of what lay beyond it, and suddenly as I stared it began furiously to pluck and tear at its breast with its taloned foreclaws.

"So frenzied were the creature's exertions that the front of its space-suit came away in shreds. The hideous creature had scales on its breast instead of feathers, and a pulsing, lizardlike throat ... a throat which turned red as it continued to inflict cruel injuries on itself.

"The impression I got was one of agonized despair, of a creature trapped and cornered that could only escape by destroying itself. Again and again it slashed at its flesh, twisting about in the glow, its eyes brimming with agony.

"Then, suddenly, it was no longer alone. A little bird-lizard shape had materialized at its side and was going through the same grisly pantomime.

"As I blinked in stunned disbelief a third shape swam into view—and a fourth. The eyes of the third shape were dull and opaque, like frosted glass, and the fourth shape was so atrophied that the scales on its breast seemed to overlap, squeezing out the flesh between them.

"Then, abruptly, the first shape began to grow transparent. It shriveled and glistened, and I could see its skeleton gleaming beneath the glassy transparency of its dissolving flesh.

"It vanished in a gush of gray light, so quickly that the air about it had a sucked-in look. Swiftly, terribly, the other shapes converged toward that swirling vacuum and were swallowed up, as though with their passing Time had collapsed in upon itself.

"That Time *had* collapsed I knew! For I am no fool. Long ago the alien inhabitant of another world had landed in that valley of all horror, and the living shuttlecock had split it up into time fragments, the better to destroy it.

"It wanted me to know that—to realize that my time was short. So it had brought back a scene out of the past to unnerve me, and sap my will!

"Could I go on taking it? I hadn't much time to think about it—for the web was filling with another picture. A living shuttlecock, the old one had called it. So now it was weaving another picture for me on Time's dissolving loom.

"It was a picture so hideous I could hardly bring myself to believe in it. It was a picture of still another me. But if the old one had seemed palsied, wretched, at the end of his endurance—the face that stared out at me from the radiance was a thousandfold more so!

"It was a face that had lost itself in Time—a face that was all sagging jowls and puckered brows, a toothless, yellowed caricature of a face.

"But it was my face still—*my* face ravaged by a century's decay!

"Looking at myself as I would be—I suddenly had no longer any desire to live. A small, shrill voice shrieked within me that the monstrous, living shuttlecock desired just that—that it was resorting to a devilish subterfuge!

"But I did not heed the voice. I just stood there, waiting to die, hoping that the end would come quickly.

"The blast was deafening! The sudden crash of it made a muffled booming in the thin air, and smashed against my eardrums like a trump of doom. The flare was blinding. The awful brightness of it lit up the cave like a hundred suns, and burned through my eyeballs into my brain.

"When the smoke cleared all I could see at first was a shattered something lying on the floor of the cave, all twisted and bent back on itself like a smoking heap of shattered glass.

"As I shook my big, dull head to clear it my boy-self lifted off his helmet and returned his blaster to the holster on his hip. His face was shining with triumph. The sweat was running off it and he was breathing heavily.

"But he spoke to me and his words were good to hear.

"'We got him, pal!'

"He didn't say 'it'—didn't refer to the monstrous creature as something unspeakably alien.

"No—why should he? To him it wasn't a horror in the valley of the moon. It was something out of a nightmare and he knew he'd wake up safe in his own little bed at home.

"He was still thinking of me as his father—in a nightmare. We'd been hunting jabberwocks together!

"And that lad was still in me—a part of me! I tell you, it sobered me and made me feel ashamed.

"I was still feeling ashamed when both the boy and the old one vanished. Perhaps melted back would be a better way of putting it. For they did seem to dissolve and flow back, rush back, into me an instant before I found myself standing alone again—in that valley that would never grow old!"

Charley had arisen and was standing by the fire. Suddenly he stooped and threw another log into the flames.

Far to the west the lights of the biggest spaceport on Earth blinked through the purple haze, and every time a ship took off, bound for the great outer planets, the desert would light up for miles.

But that light couldn't hold a candle to the one that blazed in Charley's eyes.

Milton Keynes UK
Ingram Content Group UK Ltd.
UKHW010839190424
441445UK00004B/343

9 789357 937535